The Princess and the Café on the Moat

and the

MARGIE MARKARIAN · ILLUSTRATED BY CHLOE DOUGLASS

PUBLISHED BY SLEEPING BEAR PRESS

To Richard, my knight in shining armor,
and Rebecca and Peter, my happily ever after.
–MM

To the Pencil Wobblers, without their continued belief and support
none of this would have been possible!
–CD

2395 South Huron Parkway, Suite 200, Ann Arbor, MI 48104 • www.sleepingbearpress.com. © Sleeping Bear Press • Printed
and bound in the United States. • 10 9 8 7 6 5 4 3 2 1 • Library of Congress Cataloging-in-Publication Data • Names: Markarian,
Margie, author. • Douglass, Chloe, illustrator. • Title: The princess and the café on the moat / written by Margie Markarian ;
illustrated by Chloe Douglass. • Description: Ann Arbor, MI : Sleeping Bear Press, [2018] • Summary: "Thwarted in her efforts to
be involved in the palace's activities, a young princess with a kind heart and a determined spirit finds opportunities to be useful
outside the castle walls"– Provided by publisher. • Identifiers: LCCN 2017029906 • ISBN 9781585363971 • Subjects: CYAC:
Princesses–Fiction. • Helpfulness–Fiction. • Kindness–Fiction. • Conduct of life–Fiction. • Classification: LCC PZ7.1.M3716
Pri 2018 • DDC [E]–dc23 • LC record available at https://lccn.loc.gov/2017029906

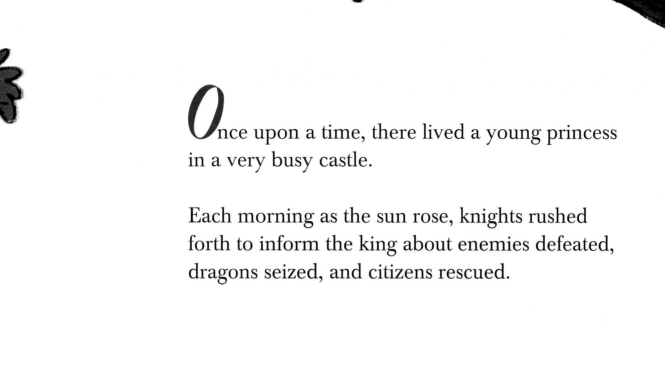

Once upon a time, there lived a young princess in a very busy castle.

Each morning as the sun rose, knights rushed forth to inform the king about enemies defeated, dragons seized, and citizens rescued.

Upstairs, ladies-in-waiting crowded around the queen, counting silks to sew, invitations to ink, and chandeliers to shine.

The princess wanted to be part of the bustle, too.
But her eager efforts went unnoticed, her sweet voice unheard.

So she roamed the castle on her own, looking for ways to keep busy.

She came upon the *court jester* juggling in the courtyard.
But he did not have time to teach her his tricks.

"I must perfect my act for our evening guests,"
he explained.

She heard the *wandering minstrel*
playing his mandolin atop a balcony.

He called down, "Your fingers are too
delicate to pluck these wiry strings."

She smelled spicy potions brewing in the tower.

The *wise wizard* shouted, "Come no closer!
It is too dangerous for you to join me."

As she passed the royal bakeshop, the princess remained hopeful. *Maybe the* royal baker *will let me frost the cupcakes or fill the fruit tarts*, she thought.

But alas, the royal baker shook her head and said, "My sticky, steamy bakeshop is no place for a young princess."

And so it continued. No matter where the princess went in the very busy castle, no one wanted her help. No one had time to teach her a new skill.

The princess's kind heart and eager spirit were not easily discouraged.

As she neared the castle's front gates, the princess said,

"Maybe there are people outside the castle who would welcome my help. If only the castle walls were not so high, and the moat not so wide and deep, I could find out."

And just as the princess spoke these words, the drawbridge magically descended . . .

the guard momentarily turned away from his post . . .

and the princess dashed across
the bridge, unnoticed and unheard.

Upon reaching the other side of the moat, the princess saw a sad *old man* holding a scrolled parchment.

"Sir," said the princess, "what brings you so much sadness on this sunny day?"

The old man replied, "My eyesight is weak and I am not able to read this letter from my son who is so far away."

"I have time to read your letter and sit awhile," said the princess, happy to have found a task so quickly.

Next, a *worried widow* with five children passed by.

"Madam," called the princess, "what troubles you so on this sunny day?"

"Now that my husband is gone, I must travel to the village marketplace to sell these fresh fruits," said the widow.

"But my children are too young to leave home alone. This is a long journey for them. They are tired, but we cannot stop to rest."

"I'd be happy to watch your children while you make your way to the village," said the princess.

A while later, a *brave squire* limped by the place where the princess, the old man, and the widow's children were telling stories and playing games.

"Brave squire," called out the princess, "what pains you so on this sunny day?"

"I gashed my knee in a skirmish many miles ago but have not stopped to tend to it," said the squire. "I wanted to get back to the castle without delay."

"You are not far from the castle now, so surely there is time for me to clean and bandage your injury," said the princess.

As the princess tended to the squire's wound, there was a sudden uproar at the very busy castle.

The king and queen were in a panic. With their daily duties now complete, they realized that they had not seen or heard the young princess all morning.

The alarm was quickly sounded. But no one, it seemed, knew where the princess was.

Just then, the sounds of laughter and song could be heard in the distance. They wafted in from the clearing on the other side of the moat.

"Could it be our princess?" asked the king as he peered out a turret window. "Yes, indeed!"

Everyone hurried to the front gate.

They scurried across the drawbridge.

They raced to the young princess and her companions.

The princess could not help but hear all the commotion. She waved and said excitedly, "Mother, Father! At last, I have found a way to keep busy, too!"

She told them how much she enjoyed reading the letter for the old man, watching the widow's children, and tending to the squire's injuries.

And although the king and queen were quite upset that the princess had wandered from the castle grounds, they were proud to have such a kindhearted daughter.

"My dear daughter," said the king, "I am relieved that you are safe, and I see that you have befriended some of our loyal citizens. Let us all celebrate together with treats and refreshments."

"I know the perfect spot," added the queen. "And I know the perfect way to keep our princess as busy as she wants to be."

$\mathcal{A}$nd from that day forward, from noon to sunset . . .

The drawbridge came down, tables and chairs were set up, and the young princess welcomed townspeople and travelers from far and wide to her café on the moat.

And in this busy, joy-filled place . . .

The *court jester* perfected his juggling.

The *wandering minstrel* made merry music.

The *wise wizard* prepared refreshing drinks.

And the *royal baker* served her tasty treats.

The *old man* made many friends.

The *worried widow* relaxed.

The *brave squire* continued protecting the kingdom.

And the king and queen always found time to stop by.

Indeed, they all lived
happily and *busily* ever after.

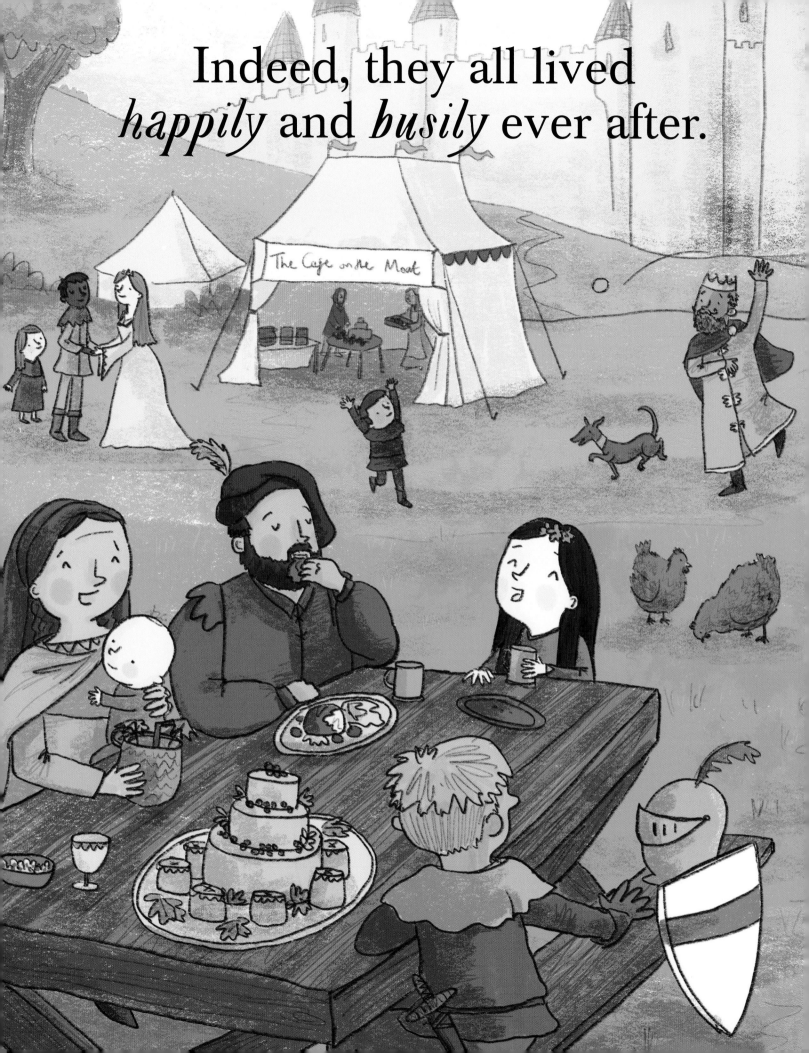

About Fairy Tales . . .

Fairy tales are a type of fiction, or make-believe, story. Like most fairy tales, *The Princess and the Café on the Moat* begins with "Once upon a time" and ends with "happily ever after." There's also a castle, royalty, and a little bit of magic. The actions in fairy tales often take place in a series of three events. This story includes several series of events. How many can you find? Look for a series of four events, too.

Fairy tales often have "good" characters versus "evil" characters, as well as a problem to solve. The characters in this particular fairy tale are mostly good, especially the princess. But she definitely has a problem. So does the kingdom. What do you think the problems are?

Fairy tales have a message or moral. I was inspired to write this story because I wanted to spread a message about responsibility, kindness, and community. Each of us has the ability to improve the places where we live, work, play, and learn. Being kind, helping others, sharing our talents, and taking time to be together are easy ways to start. The young princess knew this and discovered ways to make a difference. Ultimately, all the citizens in her kingdom—young and old, big and small, mighty and weak—came around to the princess's way of thinking, too, and followed her lead. *—Margie*

Activity: One Good Deed Leads to Another!

In *The Princess and the Café on the Moat*, the princess's good deeds create a chain reaction of good deeds in her kingdom. You can start a kindness chain, too. Here's how!

Materials: construction paper, scissors, marker, glue stick or tape

1. Cut up vertical strips of colorful construction paper (approximately 1" x 11").
2. Do something kind or helpful for a friend or family member.
3. Examples: set the table, share a toy, feed the dog, compliment someone, empty the recycling bin, make a get-well card for a sick friend or relative.
4. Write down the good deed on one of the strips of paper.
5. Glue the two ends of the paper together. This is the first link in your kindness chain.
6. Continue performing and writing down the kind and helpful acts you do.
7. Add a new link to your chain each time. Remember to weave the new strip through the first link and then glue or tape the ends together. The writing should face out for easy reading.
8. Invite family members or classmates to join you in performing good deeds.
9. Each person adds new links to the original chain.
10. You will all be amazed at how quickly the chain grows.

Congratulations! You are helping to make your world a better place.